THE ELEPHANT BOX

By

Kelly Namey

Published by Little Studio Films

ISBN: 979-8-9930592-3-5
LCCN: 2025922710

Edited by: Heidi Stangeland
Cover by: Heidi Stangeland

Dedication

For my mother, the rock of our family.
She wore life adorned with pearls of laughter, strength, and unconditional love.
A hundred pounds of vivaciousness carried the hidden weight of losing her sons and daughter.
Time did not heal her; the *WHAT IFS* became the quiet triggers of her dementia.
Cherished memories slowly intertwined with painful ones, fading together.
Her words remained locked within the prison of her mind - except for three that would escape from time to time:
"I love you."

Contents

THE LAST CARD

It was a soft spring night in Pittsburgh's South Side — the kind that teased summer and made the city's steel bones seem almost tender. The Pittsburgh air, still thawing from winter's bitterness, rolled down the Monongahela with just enough warmth to unbutton blouses and loosen collars.

An up-tempo Italian love song hummed from a passing car stereo, floating past the bright marquee of the neighborhood theatre:

CONGRATULATIONS
SOUTH SIDE'S 1981 GRADUATES!

South Side buzzed like a jukebox. People filled the streets — women with big, teased hair, men in disco suits channeling Travolta swagger, their laughter bouncing between the narrow brick buildings washed in neon lights. They spilled from nightclubs and trattorias, carrying with them a restless energy. Inside one of the more raucous haunts, Giacinta's Italian Cuisine, a live band thumping a bassline, played that same Italian love song to a packed crowd beneath a haze of cigarette smoke.

The kitchen rattled with noise and steam, as if the building itself were alive with appetite. Pots clanged, sauce bubbled, and the scent of garlic and oregano clung to every brick.

In the dim back room, away from the clink of glasses and the swirl of dancers, Benito "Beans" Moretti played a poker machine like an instrument. Dressed in a velour tracksuit, Beans was a man both toughened and tired — a fixer by nature, a man with more regrets than confessions.

The machine blinked. Two queens. Two kings. The final card hung in a stubborn freeze, daring him.

"Come on, you sonofabitch," he muttered, tapping the side. Nothing. He slaps it again--- firm, mechanical, like a man who knew where to hit life to make it work.

The machine chirped. A third queen dropped into place.

A full house. Damn right.

Behind him, laughter rolled from the poker table, where men with guts and grudges wagered more than cards. Beans barely noticed. His mind was elsewhere---on the knife he kept tucked in his sock, on the smell of lemon-scented cleaner failing to mask the evidence of decay.

Gia, the owner, bustled past carrying an oversized box of Borax and a bag of sugar, sweat on her brow, and a bandana in her hair like Rosie the Riveter reborn.

"What's the deal, Gia?" Beans asked, eyebrow cocked.

She leaned close, eyes darting.

"Cock-a-roaches," she whispered.

Beans followed her nod to a huge one scaling the wall. With zero ceremony, he reached into his sock, pulled out a blade, and flicked it. The roach dropped with a splat.

"Problem solved," he said, deadpan.

Gia chuckled, half amused, half appalled. Beans just shrugged and joined the table of poker players — Ricco among them, the kind of weasel whose smirk begged for a smack.

"Retirement doesn't suit you," Ricco sniped.

Beans didn't flinch.

"Six machines are down," Ricco continued. "Marco's losin' money. Hired some idiot who doesn't know what the hell he's doin'. Not like you. Marco doesn't like losin' money."

"I could not care less."

Ricco leaned in, smug.

"You're such a shithead, Beans."

Beans sipped his whiskey. "And you're holding a pair of threes."

Laughter scattered around the table. Ricco glowered.

Gia caught Beans' eye and winked.

Beans stood.

"I got a project," he said.

"A project?" Ricco sneered. "Is that what you're callin' her these days?"

Beans paused. The love song stops. Ricco shoved in his chips. Bluffing, everyone knew it.

Beans smirked. "That pair is as pathetic as you are, Ricco."

Someone called Ricco's bluff.

Ricco glided his fingers through his slicked-back hair and caught Gia's amusement. Beans left with the hum of the love song still drifting through the walls---his mind on the project awaiting him in his workshop at home.

THE PROJECT

By daylight, the Moretti home sat proudly on its quiet street like a guardian of old traditions. A stately two-story brick, tucked into one of Pittsburgh's finer neighborhoods — a far cry from the smoky chaos of Giacinta's. The yard was manicured with precision, framed by a hundred-year-old maple that rustled in the soft breeze, and a porch large enough for neighbors to share coffee and gossip.

Two vehicles stood in the driveway: a brand-new Chrysler gleaming under the sun, and a hulking 1979 Winnebago, wood blocks behind the back tires, still boasting its price tag on the windshield. The motorhome's wood paneling and STEELERS bumper sticker gave it a homespun charm. The license plate read: MORETTI — no mistaking who lived here.

Behind the house, tucked away from view, Beans worked alone in his shop. The space was a tinkerer's dream — part garage, part sanctuary. Tools hung from pegboards in meticulous order, alongside old slot machines and parts, photos from a younger, hungrier time, and a dartboard peppered with knife scars.
At the center of it all, perched at his worn workbench, sat a puzzle box — its wood rich and dark, the grain so smooth it shimmered under the overhead light. Beans' hands moved with delicate precision, carving intricate grooves into the lid. Sweat beaded on his forehead, not from heat, but from memory.

His eyes drifted across the room to two photographs
pinned above his bench. One showed his son, Tony,
holding hands with his wife, Anna, dressed in a
waitress uniform, inside Marco's Restaurant, where
Beans had worked. The other was his beloved,
Chicky, in her kitchen, ladling sauce from a pot,
caught mid-laugh, the light bouncing off her cheek
like a spotlight.
Beans stared at them for a long moment, then wiped
his blade clean and ran it down a leather strap with the
care of a surgeon. The blade sang against the strop.
He turned back to the puzzle box.
This one had to be perfect.

The inside of the home had seen births,
funerals, and everything in between. Every scuff on
the banister, every rosary draped over a nail carried
memory. The scent of brewing coffee mingled with
the scent of wood dust and garlic--- the Moretti
family's perfume of legacy.

In the kitchen, Carmen 'Chicky' Moretti was on
a mission. She searched the kitchen drawer for her
notebook, muttering about the week's grocery list.
Instead, her fingers found a photograph.
Its edges curled, its colors faded — but the subject
was clear. Anna, on her wedding day. Her veil lifted
in the summer breeze, her laughter caught mid-burst.
She looked like sunlight captured on film.
"She was beautiful," Chicky whispered. "Like an
angel in white."

Containers of sauce, lasagna, chicken cutlets, and other carefully labeled meals were stacked high inside the freezer. Her small frame moved rhythmically as she counted them aloud under her breath, once, twice, three times, on the notepad covered in digits by the fridge---this wasn't her first. Again. And again. Losing track, she started over.

Back at his workbench, Beans was on a mission of his own. Sawdust drifted like snow, clinging to his shirt. He sanded the edges of the puzzle box until they were smooth as glass. But when he looked down at the piece of wood, all he saw was Anna's smile, framed in sunlight.

Later, at the dinner table, Beans leaned back in his chair, a satisfied smile on his face as he admired his finished box. Across from him, Tony — now in his forties and reeking of rust belt mentality — shoveled food into his mouth with practiced efficiency. His own son, Carman, sat beside him, flipping through college brochures from *Pitt* with one hand and spearing sausage with the other. Chicky serving them as always. All that mattered to her, sitting at her table.
Beans tapped his glass.
"Sit down, sweetheart."
Chicky wiped her hands on a dish towel, her movements precise, then joined them.
With a little ceremony, Beans pushed the puzzle box toward her.

"What do you think, sweetheart?"
She looked at him, eyes wide. She'd always known when he was proud of something — it curled into his voice like a second heartbeat.
"It's a puzzle box," he said. "You gotta make a bunch of moves — that opens the lid."
Chicky ran her fingers over the smooth wood, tracing the carvings as if reading braille.
"It's what ya call a brain teaser."
She stared at it, then at him.
"Oh my," she said.
Tony groaned. "Are you kiddin' me?"
"What's your problem?" Beans shot back.
Chicky silenced them both with a gentle hand.
"It's beautiful," she said, voice soft as linen.
"*Amore mio...*" she whispered and cradled the box like a child.
Tony rolled his eyes and stood up.
"Yinzer wastin' yer time. I'm goin' ta work."
Neither of them responded. Beans just watched Chicky, his jaw softening.

THE SAVANT

Late that night, the Moretti house was quiet, save for the hum of the refrigerator and the distant crooning of a love song drifting in from someone's radio. In the living room, a single lamp glowed beside an old armchair, throwing soft light across the walls lined with black-and-white photos and framed prayers.

Chicky sat curled in that chair, her glasses perched on her nose, her gaze locked on the puzzle box resting delicately in her lap.
She turned it slowly, studying its edges with the curiosity of a child. Her fingers traced each groove, each notch — feeling more than just wood and craftsmanship. Beans had called it a brain teaser, but there was something deeper inside this box. She could feel it.
She began to work it — gently sliding a panel, then another. Her movements were hesitant at first, then faster. The room stayed silent, her breath soft and shallow. Time slipped away.
A quiet click.
The lid opened.
Chicky blinked at the open box in her hands, astonished.
And then, her eyes fluttered shut.
Beans entered the room sometime later, rubbing the back of his neck. A poker machine buzzed quietly in the kitchen; unfinished drinks sat on coasters. But his

eyes fell instantly on Chicky, dozing in the armchair, and the box, now open, beside her.

His jaw dropped.

"No way..."

Headlights flashed up the driveway. Beans scrambled, picking up the lid with trembling hands. He reached to touch her — and she startled awake, gasping.

"Chicky, honey, it's just me," he said.

Tony stormed through the front door, rake in hand, ready for war.

"What's goin' on?" he barked. "She was screamin'!"

"She wasn't screamin'!" Beans snapped back.

"This—" He shoved the lid at him. "This was for your mutha!"

Carman came bounding down the stairs, hair tousled from sleep, wide-eyed.

"What the hell?"

Beans held the puzzle box lid like evidence in a trial.

"You do this?" he asked Carman.

Carman shook his head, baffled.

Beans turned back to Chicky, barely able to contain his amazement. "I can't believe she did it so fast. There's nothin' wrong with her."

"Enough, Beans," Chicky said quietly, standing.

She gathered herself with the grace of a woman who had long learned to carry everyone else's burden.

"When the time comes, you boys will need to handle things better."

She started up the stairs, leaving the box and the chaos behind.

"I'll fill the freezer," she added, half to herself. "At least we won't starve to death."

Sunday mornings carried a ritual. The smell of simmering sauce, the clatter of pans, the radio playing Sinatra. But Chicky moved through the kitchen like a ghost, forgetting steps, repeating questions.
"Where's the basil?" she murmured to herself.
She landed at the stove, stirring the pot with mechanical rhythm, her eyes distant as she tasted the spoon and muttered to herself.
Tony wandered in wearing a baseball uniform, Carman close behind, still adjusting his shirt and draping a tie loosely around his neck.
"Smells like Alfonsi's," Tony said, kissing his mother's cheek.
"Fresh sausage," she confirmed, stirring once more.
As if by habit, Chicky reached for Carman's tie and attempted to help, but her hands fumbled the knot. Carman gently smiled and finished it himself.
"Where's Nonno?" he asked.
Chicky hesitated, searching for the answer in the sauce.
"He's... I don't know."
Tony nodded toward the back. "Check the workshop. He's goin' nuts with them stupid boxes."
Carman bent to kiss Chicky's hands.
"Can't take you to college with me, Nonnina," he said, smiling. "Which sucks, 'cause no one cooks like you."
He left for a job interview, adjusting his tie as he went. Tony followed, kissing Chicky's temple.

"Smells great, Ma."

That night, Carman and Beans sat in the living room, a small pile of puzzle boxes on the table between them — every one of them opened. Chicky sat nearby, another box in her lap, her fingers flying as if possessed. Click. Slide. Twist.
Another lid popped off.
Beans shook his head in awe.
"She's like a savant or something."

THE LEGEND OF THE ELEPHANT BOX

In the dark, back in the workshop, Beans carved furiously, blood blooming across his fingers from a fresh cut. The box on his bench was still unfinished, still flawed.

Tony appeared in the doorway.

"It's almost midnight."

Beans didn't look up. "Mind your own business."

Tony stepped inside, spotting the blood.

"What the hell happened? You drunk?"

"I'm fine."

"You're bleedin' all over the place."

"I said I'm fine."

Tony stared at his father — the bandaged hand, the tight jaw, the raw edges.

"I got a couple hours to crash before work," he muttered. "Ain't wastin' it talkin' sense into you."

Beans turned toward the door, pausing.

"She's mournin' too."

Tony didn't respond. Then, the knife in Beans' hand slowed.

Just for a second.

The next day, Beans and Chicky prepared to leave in the Chrysler. Beans' hands were bandaged from the rare cut in the workshop. Carman was across the street, pushing the mower through the grass in front of D'Angelo's Funeral Home.

Dominic D'Angelo, keeping one eye on the *new hire* manicuring his lawn, read the paper with a cigar dangling from his lips.
Tony leaned against the Chrysler, arms crossed.
"Dominic'll work him hard," he said, nodding at Carman.
Beans picked up a baseball and hurled it at his grandson, who didn't look up.
"Let's go!" he shouted.
Tony raised an eyebrow. "Wait. What?"
"He's comin' with us."
"He's workin' here!"
"Lighten up. Dom ain't gonna fire him."
Carman jogged over, hair damp with sweat.
"Let's roll."
Tony stepped closer to Beans, muttering low.
"You're crazy."
Beans grabbed Tony's collar gently, pulling him close.
"I don't like that word. Understand?"
Tony nodded. "Sorry, Pop."
Beans released him and patted his cheek.
Chicky leaned over to the window. "Don't pick, you'll ruin your supper."
Beans gave a short wave to Dominic as they pulled out of the driveway.
"Thanks, Dominic!"
Tony watched them disappear down the block, then threw his glove to the ground.

The bell above the door jingled as Beans pushed into Puzzles 'N More, a musty little novelty store tucked between a thrift shop and a check-cashing place. The floorboards creaked. Every inch of the shop was packed with curios — lava lamps, oddball puzzles, vintage games, incense sticks, and a life-size cardboard cutout of Elvis Presley giving a lazy wink from the back wall.

Behind the counter, a young woman glanced up, cigarette hanging from the corner of her mouth. She couldn't have been older than nineteen. Punky hair, guarded eyes, chipped black nail polish. Her name tag read: LEIA.

Beans tilted his head.

"Hi, Leia. As in Princess?"

Without missing a beat, she replied, "Last I saw my mom, she was suing George Lucas."

Beans chuckled. "Got any puzzle boxes?"

Leia took a slow drag.

"Nope."

He sighed, disappointed. "All right. Thanks."

But as they turned to go, she called out. "Wait."

Leia rifled through a cluttered back counter, muttering to herself. Finally, she held up a folded newspaper. She opened it to a feature article and slid it across the counter.

Carman read aloud:

"A legendary African puzzle box goes to auction in Philly a week from Saturday..."

Beans perked up.

"Let me see that."

Carman handed it over. Beans' eyes landed on a photo — the box carved into the shape of an elephant.

He showed it to Chicky, who smiled faintly, her fingers brushing the image.

Leia leaned on the counter, watching them.

Carman kept reading:

"According to the Associated Press, this intricate puzzle box carries with it a mysterious legend. If anyone opens the lid, they'll be rewarded with a memory as long as an elephant's."

Beans scoffed. "And my ass smells like flowers."

"Let him finish, Beans," Chicky said gently.

Leia raised an eyebrow. "Okay with you, Chuckles?"

"Please," he said, waving her on.

Carman continued:

"The almost two-hundred-year-old box was made on Mount Kilimanjaro. It was designed by a gamba — a warrior — to hide the knife he stole during conquest. It's believed the knife is still inside."

Beans read over his shoulder now, the words slowing in his throat.

"The box will be auctioned off in Philadelphia on June 22nd. Bidding starts at one thousand dollars."

He set the paper down, staring at it like it had just offered him a second chance at something lost.

Leia watched him closely.

"You wanna hear the rest or not?"

"Sure. What the hell."

She continued:

"The warrior, the gamba, had spared an elephant named Sanbu during battle. The animal gifted him longevity and memory. The puzzle box was carved in the likeness of Sanbu. Legend says whoever opens it inherits the same."

Chicky's eyes misted. She reached for the paper again.

Beans didn't say anything. He just stared at the photograph.

As they turned to leave, Beans paused.

"That paper is from a week ago. How'd you remember it?"

Leia shrugged. "My uncle was an auctioneer. Taught me everything."

"This his store?"

"Was. He's dead. Now it's mine."

Beans nodded, letting that settle. Then: "You believe all that legend crap?"

"Doesn't matter what I believe," she said.

He looked at the elephant box again. Something in his posture shifted — that old Moretti restlessness returning.

Leia offered him the newspaper, but Beans did a quick shake of the head. No one's that gullible he convinced himself.

"Hah," he said.

As they headed for the door, Leia smiled at Carman. He smiled back.

Beans didn't miss it.

CANNOLI AND GHOSTS

Later that evening, Giacinta's buzzed with its usual Saturday night revelry. Noisy, full of clinking glasses and the scent of fried calamari. Patrons packed the tables, waiters danced between chairs, and a Sinatra tune played lazily in the background.

At a small table in the corner — set for three — Beans, Chicky, and Carman sat lingering over cannoli and digestifs. The candles flickered. A little melted wax pooled in the center of the red-checkered cloth. Chicky leaned against Beans' shoulder, her fingers laced gently with his. There was a look on her face — part contentment, part wistfulness — the kind of expression you only wore when the past sat quietly beside you, sipping wine.

"So," Carman asked, nudging his fork into a cloud of powdered sugar. "What do you think about that box?"

Beans raised a brow.

"The box or the girl?"

Carman blinked. "Huh?"

Before he could answer, Gia approached, balancing a tray of empty glasses.

"Enjoyin' your cannoli?" she asked, ruffling Carman's hair. "So handsome. You have a girlfriend yet?"

Beans chuckled. Gia gave Chicky a warm nod.

"Hello, Chicky."

Beans leaned back, grinning. "Nice crowd tonight, Gia. You get rid of them bugs yet?"

Gia rolled her eyes and pressed a finger to her lips, then vanished toward another table.

Chicky tilted her head. "Who's that?" she mouthed.

But Carman had something else on his mind. He swirled his drink, hesitant.

"What's up with Dad?" he asked softly. "He wants me to go out of state for school."

Beans set down his glass. "Your old man's just worried."

"Why?"

The question hung there. Heavy. Uncomfortable. Chicky reached across and took Carman's hand in hers.

"You may not want to leave," she said gently, "but sometimes we have no choice."

Beans looked away. He rubbed the back of his neck, his thumb catching the edge of his wedding band.

Carman glanced between them. "Am I missing something?"

Beans drained the rest of his drink in one gulp.

"My Chicky," he said, voice rough. "She's the glue that keeps this family together."

"Stop," Chicky whispered, nudging him playfully.

He turned to her. "You're the yin to my yang."

She rolled her eyes. "You stubborn..."

Carman, trying to lighten the moment, shrugged. "Change is hard when you're old. I get it."

Beans shot him a look sharp enough to slice prosciutto.

"What?"

In the car ride home, Chicky dozed, her head tilted against the window. The dashboard was lined with stuffed elephants, gifts from Beans over the years, now a quiet army of memory.

A bump in the road stirred her, and she immediately noticed Carman was not in the back seat. Beans glanced at her. "I kicked him out a while back. Don't worry. He's by a pay phone."
She shot him a glare that could melt steel.
"What?" He said, picking at his teeth. "Shoulda got a toothpick. Cannoli got stuck."
She folded her arms and looked out the window.
He sighed," Not this time."
She quickly pointed out, "It's Saturday night. And I might not be in the mood."
And he made a hard U-turn.

Back home, Carman and Chicky swept into the house, silent. Straight upstairs. Beans dropped onto the couch next to Tony, who sipped an Iron City beer and watched the Pirates lose again.
"Stop dragging him into this," Tony muttered.
Beans reached for to turn off the TV. "Like Anna?"
Tony inhaled sharply.
Chicky's voice floated from the top of the stairs. "Beans?"
After making love, Beans confessed to Chicky he's human. "Maybe Tony's right?"
Chicky rolled towards him, fixated on his grief. "You still miss her?" He wiped away her fresh tear. "Every day. Just like you."

WILLING SUSPENSION OF DISBELIEF

Chicky stood at the stove with a wooden spoon circling slowly through a pot that wasn't there. Her gaze drifted past the steam-stained window, past the tomatoes ripening in the garden, to the framed picture of Tony and Anna hanging on the wall. The sight of her smiling face pinched something deep in her chest. If only Marco had not made her take the backroom cash to a separate bank on the other side of town. If only Beans had never agreed to hire her or stopped Marco from putting his daughter-in-law in danger to cover up his illegal gambling side business.
She should have insisted on that.
"*Honey?*"
Beans' voice startled her. She turned quickly; ladle clutched in her hand as though she really were cooking.
"There you are!" she said brightly. "Come stir this—I have an errand to run."
He walked to the stove, puzzled, as she pressed a kiss to his cheek and thrust the spoon into his palm.
"I'll be right back." She grabbed the car keys, purposeful in her stride.
"Don't be long," he said.
But when he looked down, reality crashed into him. The pot on the burner was empty. His stomach dropped. He flicked the knob off and stumbled into a chair, burying his face in his hands as they shook.

By the time he lifted his head again, Chicky was halfway to the car.

"Chick!"

He bolted outside, catching the door just as she was about to slam it.

"What's the matter?" she asked, brow creased with confusion.

"Ah—" He faltered. How could he say it?

"Hurry, before it burns!" she urged.

His heart broke. This was the hardest thing he had ever faced.

"Scoot over, sweetheart."

She slid across the seat, still searching his face. "What's the matter?"

He sat beside her, trying to steady his voice. "One time, I stole my Nonno's car. I was too small to push the gas hard, got caught before I got anywhere." He looked at her tenderly. "And maybe hurt someone." He reached to brush her hair from her face. "There's no sauce, honey."

Her cheeks flushed with shame. "Why is this happening?"

"It's okay." He gently took the keys from the ignition and brushed away her tears. She laid her head against his chest, trembling, and he kissed her hair.

"I'll fix this," he whispered.

"I'm not a poker machine," she murmured, voice breaking. "You can't fix me with spare parts."

He didn't believe in magic. But he believed in her. And something was slipping. Fast.

The doctor's office smelled faintly of disinfectants and old coffee. Beans stood rigid by the window, staring out at the parking lot as if he could will himself away. Chicky sat across from Dr. Ray Cavicchia, an old family friend whose nameplate gleamed on the desk.

"Beans," Ray said, "sit down. You're makin' me nervous."

With a grunt, Beans obeyed, sinking into the chair beside Chicky.

Ray sighed. "Start thinking next steps."

"Next steps," Beans echoed flatly.

"Yes."

Chicky's hand clutched his. Ray's voice softened. "For your safety and comfort, Chicky."

Beans shot to his feet, fury flashing in his eyes. "You ready?" he snapped at Chicky, already striding for the door. "Kiss my ass, Ray!"

But Chicky lingered, voice calm. "There's a nice place on Elm. They have a room open starting next month. See what you can do."

She touched Ray's manicured hand with a faint smile. "Say hi to Maria."

Ray cleared his throat. "We divorced years ago, Chicky."

She gave a little laugh, awkward and misplaced. "Ah. I never liked her."

The rain came down in sheets the next afternoon as the Chrysler pulled up to Puzzles 'N More. Beans squinted through the windshield, spotting a notice taped to the shop door.

An eviction.

His stomach dropped. He scoured the block, but Leia was nowhere. Later, he drove aimlessly through the city, fiddling with the radio, singing stubbornly through the static until the music disappeared.

By nightfall, he was soaked and exhausted, huddled in a phone booth. He called home. "Kiss your Nonnina for me. I'm too beat to drive." His voice cracked as he hung up the receiver.

He woke the next morning in the backseat of the car, sunlight washing over his face. Stretching stiff muscles, he approached the shop again. Through the glass, he saw the clutter still inside — puzzles stacked, shelves dusty. On the floor, just visible beneath the mail slot, lay a piece of unopened mail: addressed to Leia Rivera.

A smile tugged his mouth. He had her name.

By evening, Carman sat in the passenger seat, paper in hand. "Rivera," he confirmed, pointing down the block. Beans turned.

At an apartment building, Beans followed the sound of a bouncing basketball to the courtyard. Leia was there, cigarette tucked into the corner of her mouth, playing a casual game with a lanky young man.

"You lost, mister?" she called, not breaking her dribble.

"I'm crushed," Beans answered, stepping into the sun. Recognition flickered across her face. "Oh yeah. Chuckles."

"What happened?" he asked.

She shrugged, still dribbling.

He gestured to the boy. "Wanna give us a minute?"

Leia nodded, and the kid jogged off.

Beans stepped closer. "You shoulda said something the other day. Maybe I coulda helped."

Leia laughed, releasing a puff of smoke. "Helped?"

"That's what I do," he said simply. "I fix things."

Her lips curved. "So what, you were just gonna bail me out, 'cause that's your thing?"

"No."

She shot again. He caught the rebound, pressing. "I woulda given you the old Moretti charm, a few pointers. Things have changed, though."

Her dribble slowed. "The store's closed for good."

"I want that box," he said.

"Have at it."

"We can work something out. You come with us, teach me about auctions."

She arched an eyebrow. "Why?"

"God, you're worse than my kid. Why what?"

"Why do you want it so bad?"

He studied her, then glanced up at the apartment windows. "You're crashing here with your cousin 'cause you got nowhere else to go. She doesn't want you around 'cause she's afraid her boyfriend'll look twice at you."

Leia stopped. "How'd you know that?"

"Your mail still goes to the store. And you don't have a boyfriend."

She smirked despite herself. "Not bad, old man."

Later, at the Moretti house, Leia spun an auction paddle like a baton as Carman hunched over his computer game.

"They chant real fast," she explained. "Keep the bid moving, that's how they make money. Don't get in a bidding war and know your limit."

"Whatever it takes," Beans said.

"Cocky," she teased. "I like that. Just don't get too excited — you'll drive up the price."

Carman grinned. "Nonno's kidding," he assured her when Beans muttered about waving a knife.

But when Tony came through the door, tension thickened.

"Who's this?" he demanded, eyeing Leia.

"This is Leia," Beans said firmly. "She's a guest in my house. Our house," he added quickly when Chicky corrected him.

Tony bristled. "Help you what?"

Beans led him into the kitchen, where the argument exploded. The puzzle box article slapped on the counter.

"We're going to Philly," Beans declared.

Tony laughed bitterly. "You're dragging Carman into this? He's got a job, college applications—"

"He's eighteen. It's his choice."

Tony slammed another beer, shaking his head. "Unbelievable."

SOME FRIENDLY ADVICE

The Moretti kitchen carried the lived-in scent of coffee grounds and old wood. Carman sat at the table, posture hunched as though protecting the glossy pamphlets spread out before him. The blue-and-gold crest of the University of Pittsburgh shone from the cover: *Department of Computer Science*. The brochures promised scholarships, opportunities, futures measured in lines of code instead of shifts at the mill.

Carman traced a finger over the embossed lettering, imagining a campus alive with possibility—classrooms full of machines that could change the world, libraries humming with untapped knowledge. He took a deep breath and flipped the page, his heart beating faster as though the future were something tangible he could clutch in his hands.

Behind him, Tony leaned against the counter, the phone cradled to his ear. His voice was flat, businesslike. "Thanks, Dominic," he muttered, before clicking it shut with a finality that made Carman flinch.

Beans entered just then, brushing the lost hair from his shoulders. His face carried the fatigue of too many sleepless nights.

"She's there again," Tony said darkly, nodding toward the front door.

Beans let out a long, weary sigh and walked away without answering, shoulders hunched as if the weight of it all pressed him lower with each step.

Left alone with his son, Tony's eyes fell to the brochures. He plucked one up, studied the pictures of bright-eyed students in lecture halls, and scoffed. "Computer Science?"

"Yeah," Carman said carefully, as though defending something fragile. "Pitt's got a good program."

Tony shook his head slowly, deliberately. "Nope."

Heat surged through Carman. His hands clenched into fists. "What's your problem?"

"You're goin' away," Tony said simply, as if that explained everything.

"I got a scholarship."

Tony's laugh was humorless. "Pick a state. Any state. You're goin' away. End of story."

Carman's anger burned through his chest. "What are you afraid of?"

"Listen ta you." Tony jabbed a finger at him, lips curling. "Balls usually stop growin' at your age."

The words cut, but Carman stood his ground. "It's not like I'm going to school to work in the mill."

"It's an honest job," Tony retorted, bristling.

"Grunt work," Carman said, swigging his soda as though the bitterness in his mouth could wash away the bitterness in his heart.

Tony sneered. "Don't be a girl."

The insult stung worse than he expected. Carman choked, and the words tumbled out too fast. "You named me after my grandmother."

The silence that followed was sharp, almost physical. Tony's jaw tightened. He snatched a pamphlet from the table, crumpled it into a ball, and threw it into the trash. "That was your mother's idea," he muttered, his voice low and final.

Carman stared at the pamphlets still scattered before him, their glossy covers now like open wounds.

The air inside D'Angelo's Funeral Home was heavy with lilies, wax polish, and the hushed murmurs of grief. Velvet drapes swallowed the light. A cluster of mourners clung to one another near the casket, sobbing into tissues and shaking their heads at the unfairness of it all.

And there, among them, was Chicky—her body swaying, her voice breaking into raw wails as though the deceased were her own. Her cries rose above the rest, matching the sorrow note for note, her grief unmoored and indiscriminate. If only mourning her own loss---finally.

Beans entered quietly, his face pale with worry. Dominic stood by the doorway, hat in hand, awkwardly shifting from foot to foot.

"Thanks, Dominic," Beans said over his shoulder, his voice flat with unspoken tension.

He crossed the room and placed a tender hand on Chicky's shoulder. "Come on, sweetheart," he whispered, the endearment trembling in his throat. "Let's go home."

She sagged into his touch, her sobs still echoing as he guided her away.

By afternoon, the two men sat outside in lawn chairs, the legs sinking slightly into the damp grass. The neighborhood was quiet except for the drone of cicadas and the occasional rumble of a passing car. Cigars smoked between their fingers, and a scattering of empty beer cans already lay at their feet.

Across the yard, Chicky emerged again, her thin frame burdened by a stack of dresses, colorful fabrics drooping over her arms. Without a word, she carried them next door. Their neighbor, Mary appeared in the doorway, startled by the offering, then accepted them with a nod.

Dominic raised an eyebrow. "What's she doing?"

"Mary's got some charity thing, probably," Beans said too quickly, the edge in his voice betraying him.

Dominic cracked another beer, foam fizzing at the lip. "That's a lotta dresses."

Beans cut him a glare sharp enough to draw blood. "She's a generous person."

Dominic took a leisurely sip, unconcerned. "Took the missus to Marco's last night. Lobster wasn't fresh."

Beans exhaled through his nose, irritated. "Shoulda got the mignon."

But Dominic pressed on, lowering his voice. "Joey Capro stopped me yesterday. Wanted to know why he didn't see nothing in the paper about a funeral for Anna."

Beans' entire body stiffened. His hand tightened around the cigar. "It's been a year," he snapped. "Let it go already."

"What are you mad at me for? I didn't tell him

nothin'."
Beans cracked open another beer, chugged half, and muttered, "You play?"
"Too crowded. Half the machines are down," Dominic answered casually. "Place has gone to hell since you quit."
Beans turned his glare full on him. "What?"
Dominic hesitated, but then, as though emboldened by the alcohol, he said, "Ya ever think that maybe Anna just broke somethin' in Chicky?"
Beans froze. The words felt like a punch. "What the hell you mean, broke?"
"You know," Dominic said cautiously. "Like a grief thing."
Beans' voice rose. "What are you, some psychiatrist now? Just shut the hell up."
He drained the can, crushed it in his palm, the aluminum screaming under the pressure.
But Dominic wasn't finished. "Think about it. Could be some kinna brain stress or somethin'."
The thought lodged in Beans' chest like a splinter. He didn't answer. Instead, he rose slowly, gaze dark, and walked back toward the house.
Dominic called after him, half-heartedly: "You goin' to the circus this weekend?"
Beans didn't turn around. Dominic downed the rest of his beer, the cicadas buzzing louder in the silence that followed.

Beans walked away from Dominic's voice, the words chasing him like stones thrown at his back.
Broke something in Chicky.

He tried to shake it off, but it clung to him, the suggestion worming its way past his defenses. He shoved his hands deep into his pockets and crossed the yard toward the house, shoulders squared against a world that wouldn't stop taking from him.

The Winnebago sat in the driveway like a relic of another life—sun-faded paint, dealer mats still crisp and unused on the floorboards. It was supposed to be their ticket to adventure, a retirement dream on wheels, but it had sat untouched for years, gathering dust and rust in equal measure. Now, with the hose in his hand, Beans sprayed the windshield, watching the dirt wash away in streaks. Droplets glistened in the late light like tiny diamonds.

He paused, lowering the hose, and glanced toward Mary's house. The dresses—Chicky's dresses—were gone from their closets, handed off as if she were dismantling her life one sleeve at a time. His chest constricted.

"Chicky, come to the door a sec, would ya, sweetheart?" he called, his voice carrying more urgency than he intended.

The screen door creaked open. Chicky appeared, framed in the doorway, her small form backlit by the hallway lamp.

"What's wrong?" she asked, her tone gentle but puzzled.

Beans swallowed hard, shifting on his feet. "Mary and Charlie got a dance or something this weekend?"

"I don't know, why?"

"I just seen you giving her your dresses."

Chicky's gaze fell, her voice quiet. "I doubt I'll ever wear them again."
The words landed like stones in his stomach. He turned back to the hose, the water splashing against the Winnebago's grill. He held the spray there a moment too long, as if the force of it could wash away more than dirt.

Later, inside the Moretti living room, the house was still except for the steady tick-tock of the clock and the faint rustle of newsprint. Beans sat in his worn armchair, paper spread before him. Chicky perched close, scanning the headlines without reading.
"They got some of them lilacs on sale, honey," Beans said absently, trying to keep his voice even.
"Lilacs?" she repeated, lowering her section of the paper. She looked at him, really looked, and saw the sadness brimming just beneath his stoic exterior.
She laid the paper aside and reached for his hand. "We have to talk about this."
Beans took her hand and pressed it firmly over his chest. "Feel that?" His eyes locked on hers. "Every time I'm near you. You wanna take that from me?"
Her throat tightened. She leaned into him, resting her head against the heart that still beat strong beneath his ribs.
"I wanna go to the circus tonight," she whispered.
Beans closed his eyes, inhaled the familiar scent of her hair, and nodded.

AN ELEPHANT NEVER FORGETS

The circus tent was alive with color and sound, a swirl of popcorn, sawdust, and brass music that filled the night air. The crowd roared as elephants lumbered into the ring, their great gray hides glistening under the spotlights. Chicky's face lit up, childlike wonder softening the lines of worry that so often furrowed her brow. She clutched Beans' arm, her cheek pressing into his shoulder.

"Do you remember our trip to Africa?" she asked, eyes wide, glistening with memory.

"Yeah," Beans said softly, though the memory was more faded postcard than living picture.

"They're such beautiful creatures," she whispered, her gaze fixed on the elephants swaying in unison.

She joined the wave rippling through the crowd, clapping and laughing. Beans clapped along, though his eyes lingered more on her than on the animals.

Tony, sitting nearby, leaned in, his voice low and sharp. "Maybe you should start thinkin' about a nice place."

"Maybe I stick you in a home," Beans shot back, never taking his eyes off Chicky.

"Us three don't know what she needs," Tony pressed.

"Then don't talk," Beans snapped, his jaw tight.

An elephant trumpeted, and Chicky laughed with delight, the sound like music in his ears. Beans clapped harder, forcing himself into her joy.

"I can handle things," he said under his breath, almost like a prayer.

Tony muttered something about him being incapable, but Beans refused to hear it. He would hold on to this moment, to Chicky's happiness, with both hands.

The Chrysler rolled along a narrow country road the next morning, its tires spitting up dust as the circus camp came into view. Trailers lined the field, ropes tied between stakes, and the unmistakable sight of elephants chained to trees. Their vast, patient eyes watched the world with sadness too deep for words. Chicky gripped the steering wheel tightly, her knuckles pale against the worn leather. She slowed as she passed, staring at the elephants swaying in place. Their trunks tugged weakly against their chains. A worker snapped a stick against one of their legs, and the creature let out a low, mournful trumpet.

Her breath hitched. The sound cut straight through her. She pressed her lips together and forced her gaze back to the road, the image searing into her mind.

At home, Carman sat tapping at his computer, the flicker of the monitor lighting his young face. A knock came at the door.

"Come in!" he called, without looking up.

Beans shuffled out from the kitchen, muttering about laziness, and opened the door to find Leia on the stoop, holding a book about auctions.

"You forget somethin'?" Beans asked.

She gave a half-smile, her eyes sweeping past him into the house. "Just…" She held out the book.

Beans nodded toward the living room. "He's in

there."
Leia brushed past him, and Beans called after her,
"Where's Chicky?"
Carman looked up from his screen. "Alfonsi's."
"Oh, cavolo," Beans muttered, his shoulders sagging.

Alfonsi's butcher shop smelled of raw meat and
sawdust. Chicky stood at the counter, her delicate
hands retrieving the brown-wrapped package Alfonsi
had prepared for her.
"Thanks, Alfonsi."
"Wait, Carmen, you forgot your change!" the butcher
called, bustling after her.
She smiled, her voice warm. "You have a nice day,
Alfonsi."
"You too, Carmen," he replied.
Her smile faltered as she turned away, the name
stinging her heart like a memory.

The drive back was lonely. The package of
meat slid gently on the seat beside her. At a stop sign,
she froze. The blinker clicked left. Then right. Then
left again. Her eyes darted from one side of the road
to the other, as though the world itself were asking her
to choose. Her hands trembled on the wheel.
She awkwardly smiled at the elephants seemingly
laughing at her on the dashboard. Her vision blurred.
Her thoughts slipped backward, back a year, to that
day.

The kitchen phone rang, its jangle slicing
through the ordinary clatter of dishes. Chicky wiped

her hands on her apron and lifted the receiver. She listened, her face draining of color, then clamped a hand to her mouth. The phone slipped from her fingers, dangling by its cord as she bolted out the door.

Her car tore through town, eyes scanning wildly, lungs burning with dread. Sirens flashed in the distance. Police cars. A small knot of uniforms around something on the pavement.

Chicky slammed the brakes, heart clawing at her chest. She stumbled from the car. The officers tried to wave her back, but she pushed through.

And there was Anna, sprawled in her waitress uniform, her body broken against the cruel concrete. An empty money bag lay inches from her bludgeoned body. The robber had taken more than one life that day.

Chicky wailed, collapsing onto the street beside her daughter-in-law, her cries torn from the deepest place she could know. An officer touched her gently, but it was useless. The world had ended right there in the road.

And then the realization. "My son. What will this do to my son?"

Like a whip, she snapped out of the memory. Chicky gasped, pulling the Chrysler to the shoulder, her hands trembling. She opened the glove box with frantic fingers, searching for something to steady herself.

Out fell an old brochure: *Johannesburg, South Africa.* The colors faded and the corners creased, but the elephants on the cover smiled up at her as though offering her a lifeline.

She clutched it to her chest and wept.

Through her tears, she looked up the road and once more saw the circus camp. Workers struck the elephants with poles, forcing them into formation. Their cries rose like prayers that went unanswered. Chicky covered her mouth, choking on sobs, and drove on, her vision swimming.

That night, the Moretti house was dim, the shadows long. Beans and Tony paced, the tension hanging heavy in the air. Headlights swept across the window as the Chrysler finally pulled up.

Chicky came in, thrust the wrapped meat into Beans' hands without a word, and fled up the stairs, tears streaking her cheeks.

Beans stared after her, helpless.

Later, when the house was quiet, Chicky crept down the staircase, dressed in dark clothes. She slipped through the door, her face set in determination.

On the country road, she parked near the circus camp. From the trunk, she retrieved a pair of bolt-cutters she took from Beans' workshop, the cold steel, heavy in her hands. She moved to the trees where the elephants were chained, her breath shallow, her heart racing.

Two circus workers approached her from the
shadows. She did what she needed to do.
She snapped the locks, her tears blurring the shapes of
the animals as they stepped free. A massive trumpet
split the night air.
Chicky raised her hand, waving them forward.
"You're safe now, Anna," she whispered hoarsely.
"Go."
The elephants lumbered down the road, their
silhouettes fading into the dark.
She shoved the bolt cutters back into the trunk,
slamming it shut with trembling hands. She stood
there for a long moment, tears on her cheeks, the echo
of trumpets ringing in her ears.
But nothing, not memory, not grief, not guilt, not
saving a life, could be switched off.

PHILLY

Sweat rolled down Beans' face as he stood at a bank teller's window. Was the summer heat early, or was it the pressure of withdrawing their life savings to buy into a fantasy?

That night, Beans couldn't sleep. He stood at the window, watching the Winnebago in the driveway. Chicky had packed her notebook and a small suitcase. Carman had agreed without protest, which said more than words ever could.

Across the street, Dominic D'Angelo's porch light flicked off. The street was quiet.
Beans stayed at the window, heart pounding with something he hadn't felt in a long time.
Purpose.

The next morning, the sun rose slowly and thickly over the South Side, casting long shadows across the driveway. Birds chirped like gossiping neighbors. Dew clung to the Winnebago's windshield, blurring the reflection of the old Moretti house one last time before the road took them away from it.

Beans stood outside with his hands on his hips, checking the tire pressure like he actually cared—like anything could stop him now.

Inside, Chicky packed a small cooler: provolone, olives, two loaves of Italian bread wrapped in foil, and Tupperware after Tupperware of homemade food she had labeled in Sharpie. She placed the final one inside with care and snapped the lid shut.

Upstairs, Carman threw the last of his things into a backpack, phone, headphones, crossword book, then paused at the framed photo on his dresser. It showed his mother, Anna, holding him as a baby. He touched the glass gently with his thumb.

Tony appeared in the driveway, wearing his work clothes and a face that said *I don't like this.* Chicky emerged from the house with her purse and notebook. She looked… calm. Not entirely certain, but ready. Carman followed, slinging his bag over one shoulder. Beans climbed into the driver's seat, closed the door, and fired the engine. It coughed twice, then roared.
Chicky kissed Tony on the cheek. "Dinners are in the freezer," she said.
Tony stared at her, then at the old RV as it pulled away from the curb, sputtering into the sunrise.

The Winnebago lumbered down the Pennsylvania Turnpike, its glossy panels still bearing the sheen of a showroom vehicle, though it had sat untouched for years in the Moretti driveway. The paper dealer mats were crisp and unstained, a reminder that no one had ever quite believed Beans would actually use them for their intended purpose. But now, at last, it was on the road, carrying within it two generations of Moretti's, and one unexpected passenger—on a journey that felt less like a trip to an auction and more like gambling with fate.

Beans sat shotgun, a map spread across his lap. He traced the black lines with his finger as if he could wrestle sense from the sprawling arteries of the state. Carman handled the wheel with the same earnest concentration he used when threading a computer's motherboard. His hands were steady, but his jaw was tight. Behind them, Chicky and Leia dozed in the bunks, lulled by the rumble of the road.

"We're about an hour out," Beans muttered, squinting at the map. His voice carried a mix of command and weariness, as though he were talking more to himself than to his grandson. "It's gonna be big, it's gonna be confusing. Keep your eyes open for signs and let me know when we're close."

Carman smiled faintly. "No sweat, Nonno."

But Beans could not resist pressing the point. "I mean it. Philadelphia ain't no two-bit town. It'll swallow you whole if you don't pay attention."

"Got it."

With that assurance, Beans allowed himself to close his eyes. For a moment, the tight lines of his face softened, and the sound of Chicky's light breathing behind him seemed to steady him. He let himself drift.

MEANWHILE, BACK HOME IN THE 'BURGH

The knock came hard and sudden, rattling the screen door in its frame. Tony was in the living room, slouched in a chair, wearing his work clothes with an Iron City beer in hand, flipping half-heartedly through the paper. The sound froze him mid-sip.

He rose slowly, his jaw tight, and crossed the room. Through the lace curtain, the outlines of two uniformed officers loomed against the porch light. Tony's gut clenched. He pulled open the door. "Evening," the taller officer said, his voice clipped, official. His partner hung back a step, scanning the street as if the night itself might produce trouble. Tony's shoulders stiffened. "Yinz lookin' for somethin'?" He scanned the street. "Pretty quiet street. Not much goes on to need you guys." His first thought: Marco's got busted, and they're looking for Beans.
"This the Moretti house?" the first officer asked.
"Yeah."
"We're looking for Carmen Moretti."
The words landed like a stone in Tony's stomach. His grip tightened around the edge of the door. "What for?"
The officer didn't flinch. "Can we come in, sir?"
"Uh, I don't think so. I'm on my way to work."
Tony's eyes narrowed as he stepped out onto the porch and quickly, but softly, pulled the door shut.

"Sir," the officer said carefully, "we're just following up on a crime, and Carmen was seen in the area."
Tony marched down the steps, forcing steadiness into his voice.
"I'm the only one home. You'll have to come back."
"Do you know when they'll be back?"
Tony hesitated. Lying to cops had never sat easy with him, but he wasn't about to hand his son—or so he thought. "I don't know," he said finally. "You'll have to stop later. I gotta go. I'm late."
The officers exchanged a look, the kind that carried doubts. Tony's jaw worked, grinding down the anger clawing at his chest—*What the hell did you do, son?*
The officers gave curt nods and turned, their footsteps heavy on the porch steps. The cruiser's headlights cut across the yard as they pulled away, red and blue lights briefly flashing in the windows.

Tony sat in his car long after they were gone, the evening pressing in around him. He shut the door slowly, leaning his head back against the rest. It would be his last for a while.

THE RV

When Beans woke, it was to the thundering bass of half a dozen boom boxes rattling car windows on a narrow city street. He blinked at the sight outside—brick row houses pockmarked with graffiti, sidewalks cracked like old knuckles, and figures leaning against lampposts with sharp eyes and sharper tongues.

Beans jerked upright. "Where the hell are we?"

Carman tightened his grip on the wheel. "Not sure."

"Not sure? What exit you get off?"

"It said Philadelphia."

"Philadelphia?" Beans shot him a look as sharp as his pocketknife. "It's bigger than Rhode Island! I told you to wake me when we got close."

Carman flinched. "I didn't wanna bother you."

"This bothers me!"

The sharpness of his voice roused the women. Leia rubbed her eyes and peered out the window. "Where are we?"

Beans scanned the streets. His instincts told him they had drifted far from safety. "Pull over there." He jabbed a finger toward a sagging corner store with peeling paint. The sign above it read simply *Carry Out*, as though it had long ago given up on promising anything more.

"I'll go with you," Carman offered, already reaching for the door handle.

Beans stopped him with a curt wave. From the glove box he drew a long knife in a leather sheath, its handle

worn from years of use. He slid it into the back of his pants like an old friend returning to his post.
"Stay put. Lock the door."
"Be careful, Nonno."
Beans smirked. "Always."

Inside the carry-out, the smell of stale beer and fryer oil hung heavy. Behind the counter, a clerk with a wiseass grin and hollow eyes leaned on the lottery machine.
Beans stepped up and nodded toward it. "Anybody hit last week?"
The clerk cocked his head. "You talking to me?"
Beans scanned the empty store, then gave him a flat look. "Uh-huh."
"I did," the clerk said, his smirk deepening. "But hey, who'd wanna leave all this?" He spread his arms in mock grandeur at the dingy walls.
Beans slid a twenty across the counter. "Directions to the Convention Center."
The man reached for the bill, but before his fingers could close around it, Beans slammed the knife down through the paper, pinning it to the counter like a butterfly specimen. The clerk's smirk faltered.
"It's just you and me, asshole," Beans said quietly, his eyes glinting.
The clerk swallowed, then grabbed a scrap of paper and scribbled hurried directions. Beans pulled the knife free, folding the twenty into his pocket with casual grace.
"Traffic's bad. If you go this way, you won't hit any," the clerk muttered. Beas gave him a nod of thanks and

turned to leave.

Back outside, the Winnebago still blocked the entrance to the lot. A beat-up Impala leaned on its horn, its driver's face red with rage.
"Get that piece of shit outta here, Wop!" the driver yelled.
Beans froze, his hand tightening on the bat he had just pulled from the motor home. The passenger leaned out, laughing.
"Hey! You drivin' your house so you don't forget where you live, old man?"
Beans swung the bat once in the air, a test of weight and intent. The driver's hand flashed toward his waistband, steel glinting in the sun.
And then, behind him, came the sharp sound of a gun cocking.
"Drop it, man."
Carman stood on the step of the Winnebago, both hands steady on a pistol. His voice did not waver.
"You too, man. Don't make me say it twice."
The laughter drained from the passenger's face. The driver let his pistol fall to the pavement with a metallic clatter. Slowly, grudgingly, they climbed back into their Impala.
"Now drive," Carman ordered.
The Impala squealed away, tires spitting gravel.
Beans turned to his grandson, pride flickering behind his scowl. "Let's get to the hotel. I'm starvin'." He eyed the gun. "How'd you know about that?"
Carman allowed himself the faintest grin. "Nonnina showed me."

Beans chuckled, shaking his head.

The Winnebago pushed on, merging into the thick artery of the Schuylkill Expressway, the skyline of Philadelphia clawing its way up through the haze. To Beans, the city looked like another poker table—flashy, crowded, and waiting to see who would bluff and who would fold.

It was a river of honking steel, brake lights glowing in angry red rows. Beans leaned forward in his seat, muttering curses over the clerk's punk under his breath. "That little prick."

Carman kept his focus on the lane ahead, hands rigid on the wheel. Behind them, Leia tried to smooth the tension with a sardonic laugh, but Chicky's hand found Beans's knee. She didn't speak—she rarely did anymore when he was wound this tight—but the gentle pressure was enough to calm him.

At last, the Winnebago lumbered off an exit, down Broad Street, and into the shadow of the Philadelphia Convention Center. The building was a monument of glass and stone, humming with activity. A banner stretched across the front:

PHILADELPHIA CONVENTION CENTER —
ARTIFACTS AUCTION.
PLEASE CHECK IN AT FRONT DESK.

Across the street rose a squat but busy economy hotel. Its neon vacancy sign buzzed faintly even in daylight.

Carman maneuvered the Winnebago into the lot

beside the convention center. As the engine coughed into silence, a man in a flashy suit and cuff links strutted by with a little dog tugging at its leash. His hair gleamed with product, his smile practiced like a salesman's.

"Nice Winnebago," the man called, his eyes scanning the vehicle with envy. "My wife and I've been thinking of getting one. Hotels never let us bring Barnie here." He bent to ruffle the dog's ears. "Pretty comfortable on long trips, huh? Bet you've done a few."

Beans slid from the passenger seat and shut the door with a firm hand. He was polite enough, but his patience was worn thin. "Yeah. Pretty nice ride."

"It's a beaut!" the man insisted.

"Not for sale." Beans's tone ended the conversation, but he extended his hand anyway. "Benito Moretti." The man blinked, startled by the old-fashioned directness. He shook the offered hand with a wary smile before moving on, dog trotting beside him. Beans watched him go, then muttered to himself, "Snake oil."

ON DISPLAY

That evening, the convention hall was transformed into a temple of desire. Rows of tables displayed artifacts and antiques under glass: ivory figurines, silver chalices, painted scrolls. Collectors moved among them with the reverence of pilgrims, whispering valuations and legends to one another.

The Morettis drifted through the crowd together—Beans, Chicky at his side, Carman and Leia trailing close. For Beans, the scene felt like a poker room dressed in finer clothes: everyone calculating odds, pretending not to want what they wanted most.
"Over here, Nonno," Carman called softly.
They gathered around a flyer-covered table. Carman picked one up and read aloud, his voice carrying just enough drama to draw the others in.
"It says the puzzle box has twenty-seven moves necessary to open the lid."
Beans took the flyer, his eyes narrowing. "Twenty-seven moves," he muttered. "Hell of a tease."
Carman continued: "The knife the gamba stole from his conquest is said to still be stained with the blood of Sanbu, a hundred-year-old African elephant. The legend states the warrior saved Sanbu during battle, and the elephant rewarded him with long life and the memory of an elephant."
"Respect," Beans said, almost reverently.
Carman read on: "The gamba put the knife inside a puzzle box carved in Sanbu's likeness. Whoever

opens it is rewarded with health of mind and body."
Beans and Chicky exchanged a long, weighted look.
Neither spoke the word aloud, but it hung between
them: memory.
"Woah." He lowered the flyer. "It's from the estate of
Akito Tanaka, recently deceased at one hundred
twenty-two years."
Chicky's lips parted in awe. Beans's throat tightened.
For a moment, he forgot the crowd pressing around
them.
Then Carman added, softly, "The truth about its real
powers is unknown."
Beans broke the spell with a gruff nod. "I'm starvin'.
Let's eat."

The hotel restaurant was a world away from the
noise of the convention. Heavy carpeting muted
footsteps, and soft amber light draped itself over
neatly set tables where small candles flickered inside
glass holders. Waiters moved quietly, balancing trays
of wine glasses and steaming plates of pasta, while
muted jazz floated from unseen speakers.
It was crowded with out-of-towners and locals alike,
all drawn by the comedy show slated for after dinner.
The Morettis sat at a small round table, drinks
sweating in front of them, a bowl of salted peanuts
between.

Leia slid into the booth first, crossing her legs
and leaning back with a defiant kind of ease, though
her eyes kept darting toward the lobby doors as if she
expected someone to yank her out at any moment.

Beans sat opposite her, his posture stiff. He picked up the menu but barely looked at it, his hands too restless to stay still. The puzzle box was never far from his mind, its mystery gnawing at him like hunger.

Carman sat between them, the silent bridge in a conversation that seemed perpetually one misstep away from collapsing. Chicky sat staring. Was it the overwhelming adventure?

A waiter approached. "Water to start?"

"Highball for me and a wine for the Missus," Beans said without hesitation, his eyes flicking briefly toward Leia, as if daring her to comment.

Leia smirked, resting her chin in her hand. "Far out."

The waiter nodded and slipped away, leaving them in the heavy hush of low clinking silverware and murmured conversations from nearby tables.

Beans leaned forward, his voice lowered, determined. "So, tomorrow—how do we play this?"

Leia lifted the menu just high enough to hide her smile. "We don't. You do. You want that box, right? Then you'll raise your paddle, keep your cool, and not let your ego write checks your wallet can't cash."

Carman chuckled softly, earning a sharp glance from his grandfather. Beans bristled.

Leia finally set the menu down flat, meeting his eyes square. "I think you're the kind of guy who believes a hard stare can win a war. But in there?" She tapped the folded flyer sticking out of her pocket. "Wars are won with patience, not fists and knives."

The waiter returned with their drinks, setting the glasses down gently. Beans reached for his immediately, taking a long swallow. The burn was familiar, steadying.

He set the glass down harder than he intended and muttered, "Patience, I got."

Leia lifted her glass of water, watching him over the rim as she sipped. "Guess we'll see."

Carman sat back, his gaze flicking between them, the weight of something unspoken heavy in the air. For all their sparring, he realized, both Leia and his grandfather were exactly the same: fighters, terrified of what it might mean to stop fighting.

The candles flickered between them, shadows stretching and contracting across their faces. Tomorrow would test them all.

Onstage, a comic riffed about Reagan and gas prices. Laughter sputtered through the room, loosening their mood.

Chicky leaned close to Beans, her hand slipping into his. "Do you remember our first date, Benito? It was a dinner show. You were so handsome."

Beans smiled, touched. "And you had that big beehive hairdo."

"Beehive!" she laughed, and for a moment the years fell away.

Leia, watching from across the table, whispered to Carman, "They're adorable."

Carman flushed, torn between embarrassment and admiration.

But when Chicky's laughter faltered, it collapsed into sudden sobs. Beans wrapped an arm around her, whispering, "Honey, I'm sorry. It's all right." He glared at a man across the room who had been

smirking at her. "What are you lookin' at? Want me to make you cry?"
The man turned back to his plate, cowed.

Music swelled as intermission began. Beans rose, extending a hand to Chicky. "C'mon. Let's show these young pups how to cut a rug."
They shuffled onto the dance floor. The song was slow, but Chicky couldn't quite find the rhythm. Beans felt the weight of eyes on them. He bent low and whispered, "Put your feet on mine." He lifted her gently until her shoes rested atop his, and together they swayed.
"Don't look at anybody but me," he told her. "We're the only two in the world."
She looked up at him, eyes glassy but shining. For that brief song, they were young again, two kids from Pittsburgh in love, the world's noise falling away.
Leia watched them with unexpected emotions rising in her chest. Carman, seeing her watch them, watched her instead.
That night in the hotel hallway, Beans kissed Chicky's temple. "Sweet dreams, beautiful." He guided her into the room she shared with Leia, who lingered in the doorway, and smiled at Carman.
"Night."
"Night," he echoed, too quickly.

In the guys' hotel room, Carman sprawled across one of the double beds, phone receiver pressed to his ear. The blue glow of the cheap lamp cast his face in tired shadows.

"Hey, Dad," he said softly.

On the other end came Tony's voice, already sharp. "Carman! What the hell did you do?"

Carman flinched, pulling the phone back from his ear. "Dad—"

"Answer me!"

Beans appeared in the doorway from the bathroom, toothbrush foaming his mouth, his undershirt rumpled. Carman thrust the receiver toward him like it was burning his hand.

"He's hot about something."

Beans grunted, spit still clinging to the corner of his mouth. He grabbed the phone.

"What?"

"You had to take all the money?" Tony's fury was a hammer on the line.

Beans winced. "Calm down."

"Calm down?!"

But Beans had had enough. He slammed the receiver back onto its cradle, foam still clinging to his lips.

"Ah." He turned back toward the bathroom with a dismissive wave. "What's the matter with him?"

Carman could only shrug. Beans muttered around his toothbrush, "Wonder where he gets it from."

Meanwhile, across the hall, the women's room was quieter but no less charged. Leia sat in her nightgown, flicking idly at the hotel's television remote, until Chicky's voice cut across the room.

"I've seen how you look at my Carman."

Leia froze. Chicky's tone wasn't accusatory, just blunt, unfiltered, as if her mind no longer kept gates between thought and speech. She turned her glassy eyes back to the screen. "Would you mind turning that off, dear?" Leia clicked it dark.

"No one talks anymore," Chicky sighed, climbing into her bed. "Tell me about yourself. Do you have any family?"

"A cousin," Leia admitted. "We're not close."

"Young thing like you needs family."

"I do okay."

"…Do okay?" Chicky frowned.

Leia hesitated. "My mom left with some lowlife. So… I just had the store."

"It's cool."

"Store?" Chicky blinked, confused. Then, softly, "Anna used to say that."

Leia tilted her head. "Anna? Is that Carman's mother?"

Chicky's face changed, heavy with longing. "I miss her."

Leia, suddenly tender, whispered, "Carman said she died last year."

Chicky looked at Leia, and something in her softened. "You remind me of her. She was so beautiful. Full of life."

The room darkened as Leia switched off the lamp. But Chicky's eyes remained open, wide, frightened, staring into the dark like a child.

"Good night, Chicky," Leia whispered.

"Good night, Anna."

Leia's heart squeezed. She crossed the small space between their beds, slipping under Chicky's covers. She wrapped an arm around the older woman's frail shoulders. Chicky relaxed at once, as though the months fell away and Anna was there again. Leia held her until her breathing slowed.

Far across Pennsylvania, Tony pulled his car into the steel mill's lot, surrounded by other workers trudging toward their shifts. He sat gripping the wheel, staring at the high school graduation photo of Carman tucked into the visor. His son's grin was frozen in time, full of promise.
"Shit," Tony muttered.
He slammed the visor shut, shoved the car into reverse, and peeled out of the lot. His hard hat tumbled into the back seat. He didn't care.

THE HIGHEST BIDDER

Morning brought its usual shuffle of footsteps and muffled hallway conversations. Beans, Chicky, and Leia left early for breakfast, leaving Carman to his own devices.

"You coming?" Beans asked.

"I wanna check out the pool," Carman announced, grabbing a towel.

"All right," Beans said. "Suit yourself."

He closed the door behind them. Carman exhaled, glad for the space. He stepped into the hall in his bathing suit, towel draped around his neck. The hallway smelled faintly of chlorine and stale smoke.

Two rookie Philadelphia policemen approached, purposeful and brisk. They glanced at their paper, then at the door he had just locked.

"We're looking for Carmen Moretti," one asked.

Carman shifted uneasily. "I'm Carman. Why?"

The cops exchanged a look. "Thought Captain said it was a female?" one muttered. The other shrugged, then turned him around with practiced efficiency.

"Carmen Moretti, you're under arrest. You have the right to remain silent—"

"What?!" Panic rose in Carman's chest. "For what?"

"Assault and theft," the officer said flatly.

"That's crazy! I didn't—" But the cuffs snapped cold around his wrists, cutting off his protest. Hotel guests craned their necks as he was led away, towel dragging on the carpet.

At the jail, Carman sat pale and stunned. They unhooked the cuffs, gave him his one call. He dialed home, praying for his father's voice and rubbing his wrists raw.

The answering machine picked up. Beans's gravelly voice spilled out: "It's Beans. When this thing beeps, lay it on me." The beep stabbed the silence.
"Dad! Where are you? I'm in the Philly police department! I don't know which one though—it's big here. Damn it!" The words tumbled out in desperation. He slammed the receiver down, forehead thudding against the payphone glass.

Meanwhile, Beans, Chicky, and Leia returned from breakfast to find their hotel room locked.
"Carman," Beans called, jiggling the handle. No answer. "Finish up and open the damn door!"
Still nothing.
He pressed his ear to the wood. "What the hell…"
Leia offered, "Maybe he's still at the pool?"
Beans scowled. "I gotta get in and grab the money."
He slid his driver's license between the jam and the lock, popping the door. The room was empty.

At the convention center, the auction was minutes from beginning. Chicky and Leia together mid-room, Leia twirling the bidding paddle nervously. Beans joined them, trying to mask his unease.
"Any luck?" Leia asked.
"He's probably at the pool."

"What if he can't find us?"
"He'll show up," Beans insisted.
Beans stood motionless in the crowd, arms crossed.
Chicky drifted along the rows, humming to herself.
Leia's eyes scanned the aged wonders: ivory
figurines, brass sextants, and war medals.

The auctioneer's voice crackled through a PA
system. "Ladies and gentlemen, welcome to the
Philadelphia Antiques Auction. Items 120 through
150 will be up for bid before our lunch break. The
featured artifact—a ebony puzzle box of East African
origin—will close the session."
Beans narrowed his eyes. "Featured."
Leia nudged him. "Means high bids. Better breathe,
Chuckles."

Just outside, Philadelphia swallowed Tony the
moment he arrived. The city buzzed with traffic and
voices, steel and glass crowding above him. But none
of it mattered. He had only one thought: find Carman.
He pushed through the revolving doors of the
Convention Center. The cavernous lobby rang with
echoes of chatter and footsteps, but his son was
nowhere in sight. He stalked through the floor,
scanning each face, each cluster of strangers. No
Carman. No cops. Only the hollow confirmation that
he was too late.
Leia frowned at Beans. "Did you bring the bidding
card?"
"What bidding card?"
"I told you last night. You gotta register to get one."

"Ah!" Beans threw up his hands. "I'll be back."

As he stalked toward the lobby, Tony appeared in the crowd, pale and frantic. "Ma, where's Carman?"

Chicky's face lit with relief. "There he is."

Tony ignored her smile. "Where's Carman?"

"He said he was going to the pool," Leia offered.

Tony's eyes darted to the sign posted near the back: POOL CLOSED FOR REPAIRS. His face drained of color.

"The police are looking for him!" he hissed as Beans returned.

"What for?" Beans demanded.

"Robbery and assault. You know what this'll do to his chances at school?" Tony knew Carman could either do jail time or the prison of a factory job.

Beans grimaced, torn between paternal outrage and the gnawing hunger to stay for the auction. He looked at Chicky, then at the stage where the auctioneer was adjusting his microphone. Choices pressed in from all sides.

The convention center swelled with chatter as the auctioneer tested his microphone. Rows of bidders settled into seats, paddles in hand, eyes gleaming. It was the hum of a poker table right before the first deal—expectation sharpened to a knife's edge.

Beans shoved through the crowd, clutching his newly issued bidder's card. Tony trailed behind, tight-jawed and sweating. "I got this," Tony said suddenly, stopping short.

"Okay? I'll find Carman."
"You need bail money."
"I'm using my retirement."
Beans froze. "Your what?"
Tony looked him square in the eye. "It's okay. I quit."
A beat, then softer: "Okay, I got canned."

The admission cracked something in Beans. For once, his son wasn't the hotheaded boy who defied him, but a man beaten down by grief, circumstance, and too many nights on the graveyard shift. Beans reached into his pocket with a trembling hand, peeling out cash.
"I'll take care of your mother," he said quietly.
Tony accepted the money with a nod, eyes shining with something between gratitude and defeat. "No doubt." He clapped Beans on the arm and pushed into the crowd, disappearing like a soldier off to battle.
Beans staggered back to his seat. Leia eyed him warily. "Where's Tony? Did you find Carman?"
"No." He didn't sit—he couldn't. His eyes darted to the stage.
Before the auctioneer could launch into the first lot, a voice boomed over the loudspeaker:
"Ladies and gentlemen, before we begin, there's a Winnebago with the license plate M-O-R-E-T-T-I double-parked. Would the owner please move the vehicle immediately?"
Heads turned. Leia nearly swallowed her cigarette.
"Take care of that, would ya?" Beans said, pressing the keys into her hand.
Leia stared. "What's that now? I don't know how to

drive that thing!"
"You got a license?"
"Well—yeah."
"You'll be fine." His wink was meant as reassurance but came off like a command.
Leia shook her head, handed him the paddle, and stomped off toward the door, muttering curses.
The auctioneer cleared his throat. "Okay, folks! Let's get started!"

Minutes later in the lobby, Beans paced in front of the concierge desk, waiting for a wire transfer that Marco was sending after Beans grudgingly agreed to go back to work for him in exchange. The clock ticked loud in his ears, each second another step closer to losing the only thing that might keep Chicky whole.
When the funds finally came through, he signed with a hand that trembled more than he liked. The money felt both heavy and insubstantial in his pocket, like poker chips he wasn't sure he had the guts to wager.

He returned to the hall where Chicky sat alone, her small hands folded in her lap, eyes drifting like a child's.

Outside, Leia wrestled the Winnebago's gearshift with white-knuckled determination. Horns blared as she blocked traffic. "Piece of junk!" she growled, jerking the wheel. Somehow, she coaxed the beast into a legitimate space. Her heart pounded, her palms slick, but she couldn't help laughing at herself

as she climbed out. "Uncle Hank, you'd be proud."
She lit a cigarette on the sidewalk, blowing out a
shaky plume of smoke.

Back inside, the auction was in full swing.
Numbers rattled from the auctioneer's mouth in a
hypnotic chant. Antique furniture, rare coins, delicate
jewelry—all passed beneath the gavel.
Beans hovered at the edge of the crowd, bidder's card
poised, his eyes flicking to the doors with every slam
of the gavel. Carman was out there somewhere—in a
cell, in trouble, in danger. But here, inside this room,
was the one chance he believed he had to restore
Chicky's fading memory, to give her back the life that
was slipping through her fingers like sand.
Every instinct in him screamed: fix this.
And fixing things, for Benito Moretti, always came
with a price.

The chant of the auctioneer was its own kind of
music, a fast, hypnotic rhythm. The crowd leaned
forward with each rising number, paddles flicking up
like dancers' hands. Beans had seen this before, in
different disguises—a poker table, a craps pit, a
corner bar with too much whiskey and too little sense.
It was the same hunger, the same desperate belief that
one more bid, one more dollar, would mean salvation.
Where's Leia? Can I do this without her? Then, as if
on cue, she stood next to him, grinning from success
and rattling the RV keys in his face.
Lot after lot passed. Beans' card itched in his fingers,
his knuckles tight. He barely heard the clatter of the

gavel as a vase went for twelve hundred, a rifle for three. His eyes kept darting to the catalog, to the black-and-white photograph of the elephant-shaped puzzle box. Twenty-seven moves. Twenty-seven ways back to Chicky's laughter, her sauce simmering on the stove, her memory intact.

At last, the auctioneer's voice rang out: "Next, ladies and gentlemen—lot seventy-three. A rare African puzzle box, nineteenth century, carved in the likeness of an elephant. Intricate in design, twenty-seven moves required to open."
A murmur rippled through the room. Heads craned. Even the seasoned collectors, jaded by centuries of antiques, seemed to sit straighter.
Beans rose half an inch from his chair. His throat felt dry.
The auctioneer lifted the box from its display. Under the lights, its wood gleamed dark and ancient, the ridges of the elephant's form painstakingly carved, almost alive. For a heartbeat, Beans swore the creature's wise, solemn eyes were fixed on him.
"Bidding will open at one thousand dollars," the auctioneer announced. "Do I have one thousand?"
A paddle shot up near the front. "One thousand, thank you. Do I hear twelve hundred?"
Beans snapped his card into the air. His heart thudded.
"Thirteen hundred, yes, thank you, sir. Fourteen? Fourteen hundred?"
Another bidder raised his card.
Beans's arm jerked again before he even thought.
"Fifteen hundred, to the gentleman in the back."

The chant quickened. Paddles rose like waves in a storm. Sixteen, seventeen, two thousand, twenty-five hundred. Beans' jaw set, his teeth grinding as the numbers climbed. Each time someone else claimed the prize, his pulse spiked with fury. He wasn't here to play games. He was here to win.

At three thousand, a hush fell. The crowd began to thin—the casual players, the curious. Only the serious bidders remained. Beans among them.

Beside him, Chicky's hand trembled in her lap. She wasn't watching the stage but staring off, glassy-eyed, as though she couldn't quite place where she was. Beans looked at her, and his chest ached.

"Three thousand," the auctioneer sang. "Do I hear thirty-five?"

Beans shot his paddle high.

"Thirty-five, thank you! Four thousand?"

A man across the aisle lifted his card, cool and deliberate.

Beans's jaw clenched. He thrust his card up again. "Forty-five!"

The room stirred with low whistles.

The auctioneer's voice rose. "Forty-five hundred, to the gentleman in the back! Do I hear five thousand?"

Beans's hand hovered, sweat slicking his palm. His mind spun with images—Carman alone in a cell, Tony scraping together bail, Marco's voice on the phone dripping with mockery. But then his eyes returned to Chicky, small and fragile, her memory sliding further from him each day.

What was a price, next to that?

His card shot skyward.

"Five thousand! Thank you, sir!"

The auctioneer's chant became a blur: "Five thousand, do I hear fifty-five? Fifty-five hundred? Yes, fifty-five, now six thousand—"

Beans's pulse hammered in his ears. His paddle rose again before the words had finished leaving the auctioneer's lips.

"Six thousand to the gentleman in the back!"

Gasps fluttered across the rows. Even among the wealthy and the reckless, this was no small sum. Across the aisle, a sharp-dressed bidder in gold cufflinks lifted his paddle with calm precision. "Sixty-five." It was the RV admirer.

Beans's head snapped toward him. The man didn't even look his way, his expression serene, as though buying memory itself were no more consequential than ordering dessert.

Beans felt heat flood his chest. "Seven thousand!" he barked, his paddle slicing the air.

The room rustled, a wave of whispers. Leia's eyes widened at the sight of Beans, red-faced, veins straining at his temple. He only got eight grand from Marco.

Beans quickly handed Leia the paddle. "I'll be right back."

Wait—what?! Totally shocked, she knew he had a plan, 'cause that's just Beans.

"Seven thousand! Do I hear seventy-five?"

Cufflinks smiled faintly, raising his paddle once more.

"Seventy-five hundred, thank you! Eight thousand?" Leia's hand trembled. She clenched the paddle tighter, her breath short. Her thoughts ricocheted—he could not—would not—walk out of this room without that box. She knew it.

"Eight!" she shrieked.

The crowd murmured, impressed, scandalized. The auctioneer's rhythm never faltered.

"Eight thousand, do I hear eighty-five?"

A pause. Mr. Cufflinks was holding the RV keys. A ripple of anticipation swept the room.

"Going once… going twice…" Leia gripped Chicky's hand. She blinked at her, confused, as if not fully sure why she was smiling at her.

"Sold! To the young lady for eight thousand dollars!" The gavel struck wood with a final crack. Applause scattered through the room. Beans ran back to his seat and sagged into his chair, a man both triumphant and gutted.

Leia exhaled smoke from her cigarette and muttered under her breath, "Jesus Christ, Chuckles."

Chicky leaned against him, her head on his shoulder. "Amore mio," she whispered. For a fleeting second, Beans allowed himself to believe the box really could hold back the tide of forgetting. That memory could be bought, bartered, saved.

But beyond the walls of the convention center, his grandson was still in a cell, his son scrambling for bail, the police closing in on their family. The elephant box sat under glass, waiting to be claimed, but already Beans felt the weight of it in his hands—

the cost heavier than money.

The gavel's echo still rang in Beans's ears as he followed the clerk to the cashier's table. He signed the paperwork with a shaking hand, sliding forward Marco's wire. When the receipt was stamped, he exhaled a long, uneven breath—as if the paper itself were a contract with fate.

The elephant box was placed carefully in front of him, cushioned in its display case. Beans reached out, fingers hovering, before finally closing around it. The wood was warm, alive. He felt the carved ridges of Sanbu's tusks, the tiny grooves of its ears. It was as though the elephant had been waiting for him. He turned, holding it up for Chicky. Her face softened in the way it sometimes did, a rare moment of clarity breaking through. "Bellissimo," she whispered.

THE FALLOUT

The Philly precinct was stark under buzzing fluorescent lights. The desk officer barely looked up as Tony pushed through, the envelope in his hand like a stone he couldn't put down.
"Where's my son?" Tony demanded.
"In the back," the officer said, gesturing to a narrow hallway. "Detective's questioning him now."

Tony didn't wait for permission. He shoved through the swinging door, past rows of desks and ringing phones, until he found the room.
Through the glass panel, he saw Carman sitting at a table. His wrists were cuffed, his shoulders tight, his eyes fixed on the floor. Across from him, a detective leaned forward, tapping a pencil on the folder spread between them.
"Carmen Moretti was seen near the circus grounds," the detective was saying. "Animals let loose."
Carman lifted his chin but didn't speak. His jaw was clenched, his silence deliberate. He wouldn't give Chicky up.
The detective leaned closer. "Now, the butcher down the street from the circus camp identified a female— your grandmother, Carmen Moretti—leaving his shop earlier that evening. But the officer said you identified as Carmen Moretti."
Still, Carman said nothing.
"Why is that? You telling me it was you that let them elephants free? Think long and hard about what you

sayin', son."

"Yes." His voice resolute.

The detective changed strategy. "You look like a college kid. Got a future. Don't throw that away, son."

"IT WAS ME."

"So, you clocked those circus workers with a pair of bolt cutters?"

"YES!" He shot out of his seat like a cannon and stared down the detective with the backbone of a true Moretti. "I clocked them right on the head!"

"It wasn't their heads, Carman. A lot lower, just below the waist."

In the nuts? He was floored. The detective saw him flinch. "Why don't you know where you hit 'em, Carman, huh?"

The door burst open. Tony stormed in, his voice cutting through the room. "Because yinz got the wrong Carmen."

The detective sat back, startled.

Tony slammed the envelope down on the table. "That's my son. He didn't do it. You want the truth? You're lookin' for my mother. Chicky Moretti."

Carman's head snapped toward him, eyes wide. "Dad—"

But Tony kept going, his voice fierce. "She's sick. She doesn't know what she's doin'. You let the boy go."

The detective glanced between father and son, the pencil still in his hand. Slowly, he reached for the envelope, flipping it open to see the bills inside.

Tony's chest heaved. He stood over the table, daring

the detective to argue, daring the world to take his son from him again.

"Is this a bribe, Mr. Moretti?"

"What? No, dipshit. It's bail." Tony surprised himself with that one. He tried to shrug it off. "Pff… you Philly guys. So suspicious."

THE LAST HOPE

A yellow cab lurched up to the curb, its engine coughing impatiently. Beans bent down, knees creaking, and shuffled toward the trunk to hoist the luggage.

Beans and the ladies watched Mr. Cufflinks drive away in the Winnebago. Chicky cradled the elephant box like a sleeping child. The morning had battered them, bruised them, and elated them. The prize, the hope—well worth it.

Tony's Impala peeled into the lot to break the mood.

The pendulum had swung.

Tony pushed the driver's door open before the car had fully stopped. His voice cracked against the wind. "We gotta talk."

Beans squinted, brushing his hand across his forehead. "I gotta hear this."

Tony stepped closer, lowering his voice. "Listen a sec."

"I guess it skips a generation—" Beans began, but Tony gripped his father's shoulders with startling firmness.

"It's not Carman, Pop. It's Ma."

The words hung there, heavier than the humid air.

Beans' brow furrowed. "What about her?"

Tony glanced over his shoulder. By the car, Chicky was showing the puzzle box to Carman, her voice a quiet hum, her face calm in a way that made the revelation feel even stranger.

"They got a witness," Tony whispered. "Says Ma let some circus elephants outta their cages or somethin'."

Beans blinked, then laughed. "You drinkin' and drivin'?"

"Would you listen? Remember that night she came home so late from Alfonsi's? The circus camped out just down the street."

"So what."

"One of them circus people saw her."

Beans folded his arms. "So what. She let some elephants go, so what."

Tony leaned closer. "She whacked two circus guys in the balls with a pair of bolt cutters."

For a moment, Beans' eyes glimmered with mischief. "Was it them clowns?" His laugh boomed, unrestrained. "Cause that's kinda funny."

"I'm serious."

"You're nuts!"

"The cops couldn't hold Carman and I threw them off her track, but we don't got alotta time here!"

Beans waved at his grandson. "Carman! Get over here!"

Chicky's head turned, curious, her eyes catching the tension as Carman nodded to Beans.

The Impala ate up the highway, its worn frame rocking gently with each rise and dip of the turnpike. Beans sat steady behind the wheel, shoulders squared, his Steeler's cap pulled low. His hands gripped the steering wheel tighter than they needed to, but he wasn't about to let anyone notice. The air was thick with unspoken accusation.

Beside him, Chicky leaned her cheek against the cool glass of the passenger-side window, watching the blur of trees and billboards slide by. Her eyes were far away, her mouth tugged with the faintest smile— as if she were remembering a time before all the noise, all the worry, when it had been just the family at the kitchen table eating her homemade spaghetti.

In the back, Carman slouched in the seat, arms crossed. He had his "I'm not talking" face on, the one Tony used to wear when he was Carman's age. He'd been quiet since the station, quiet since the cuffs, and the silence weighed heavier than words might have. Leia sat between him and Tony, legs tucked under her, spinning a plastic stir straw between her fingers. She glanced at Carman every now and then with that sideways smirk of hers, the one that always seemed to say, *Cheer up, kid. You're still breathing.*
Tony eyed the puzzle box perched in Chicky's lap, wondering, stressing… does he confess what he's done? Or does he let the so-called magic of the box somehow make this better?
Tony turned suddenly to Leia. "You still here? This is family business."
Carman bristled. "What's your problem?"
"Watch it," Tony shot back.
"She doesn't have anywhere to go," Carman muttered.
"Great."
Beans cut in, eyes fixed on the road. "What? You want her to walk?"

Tony stiffened, catching what he thought was a barb about Anna. "Oh, here we go! I had ta be at work!"

"Stop it!" Chicky's voice cracked sharp and maternal, slicing through the tension. Silence returned, uneasy and brittle.

Leia leaned closer to Carman and whispered, "Your dad's wired a little tight."

"Stay out of it," Tony snapped.

"Don't talk to her like that," Carman shot back.

"Don't talk back to your old man," Beans barked, without looking away from the windshield.

Tony rolled his eyes. "Thanks, Pop."

But Beans' gaze softened when he turned to Chicky. "Let me get this straight, honey… you let the elephants go because… you… wanted to… bring them… home?"

She looked away, her silence louder than any answer. "Nevermind," he muttered.

From the backseat, Carman asked quietly, "Now what, Nonno?"

Beans pressed his back into the seat. "Everything's under control."

Tony snorted. "Famous last words." His eyes darted to the box in Chicky's lap. "That the box?"

She passed it to him without hesitation. He turned it over in his hands, unimpressed. "How much you drop on this thing?"

"None of your business," Beans said flatly.

Long silence.

Then Tony leaned forward. "Wait… what happened to the Winnebago?"

Later that night, the Morettis trudged back through the front door of their house. Their steps were heavy, their bodies bent with exhaustion. Beans didn't stop moving. "Open it," he said to Chicky.

Tony groaned. "We just walked in the door!"

"When something needs done, well…" Beans' stare landed squarely on his son.

Tony bristled. "Maybe if you'd a not had my wife deal with your gambling shit—"

"That job put food on the table and a roof over your goddamn head!"

"Stop fighting!" Chicky snapped.

Leia hesitated. "Maybe I should leave."

But in unison, Beans and Tony turned sharply. "No!" Chicky, anger flickering across her face, marching upstairs, puzzle box clutched tightly. Without a word, the others followed.

Upstairs, the bathroom door clicked shut. Beans, Tony, Leia, and Carman loitered in the hallway, waiting. The house was hushed except for the faint plumbing groan of pipes in the walls. Minutes bled into hours. The hall clock ticked loudly, each second stretching thin. Leia leaned against the wall and lit a cigarette.

Tony sighed, glancing at the clock. "She's been in there two hours already."

"Shut up," Beans muttered.

Carman shifted uncomfortably. "Sorry," he said to Leia.

She grinned. "Are you kidding? Your family's hilarious."

Their eyes lingered on each other a beat too long, a smile tugging between them.

Tony caught it. "No no. You're goin' away to school, you understand?"

Beans snorted. "You knocked up Anna on your second date."

Carman laughed. "Seriously?"

The bathroom door creaked open. Chicky stepped out slowly, her face pale. In her hands was the puzzle box—still closed.

"I'm sorry, Amore Mio," she whispered, placing it in Beans' hands.

"You just need more time," he soothed. "Give her room to breathe for chrissake."

She shook her head.

"What about all the ones I made you?" His voice cracked.

Tony folded his arms. "Why are you pushing her?"

"Butt out!" Beans snapped.

"Come on, Nonno," Carman urged gently.

Beans' face flushed red. "She wiped both your asses more times than I can count. Give her all the time she needs!"

"Beans. Please." Chicky's voice was soft, steady.

He began to pace, fists clenched, his chest heaving. She reached up to stroke his face, her touch calming, grounding. "You're so worked up, Amore Mio."

"Leave me alone," he muttered, slamming his back against the wall.

"Nonno," Carman said quietly. "You made the others. She knows you like a book."

Something in those words broke him. Beans stumbled into the bathroom, collapsing onto the edge of the tub. His body shuddered, sobs wracking through him. Chicky followed, closing the door softly behind her. She sat on his lap, her arms wrapping around him.

"I'd rather lose memories than never make them," she whispered, stroking his face. Her eyes shone. "I could never forget you, Amore Mio."

He looked into her gaze, desperate. "I'll fix this, honey. I promise."

"Not this time," she said gently.

"We'll go to a specialist—"

She smiled, running her fingers through his hair.

"You're still young. Devilishly handsome."

Her hands cupped his face. "I want you to remarry."

His heart stuttered. "What?"

"I want a divorce," she teased, laughter spilling before she could stop it. He grinned despite himself. Their laughter softened into a long embrace.

"It's Saturday," he whispered.

"It's late. I'm tired." She kissed him once more.

From the hallway, Tony's muffled voice barked, "Focus, people!"

Beans sighed, splashing water over his face. "You realize we ain't had no privacy since that kid's been born?"

Then Tony's voice again, harsher: "What if she pleads insanity or somethin'?"

The word stabbed Beans in the chest. He froze, staring at the door as sirens wailed outside. Blue and red lights flickered through the bathroom window.

He kissed Chicky hard. The reality cut like a knife to the heart. Chicky's sanity took a back seat to her freedom. It was time to say goodbye, and that included Anna.

GOODBYE

The next day in the courtroom. Chicky stood beside her attorney, her small frame dwarfed by the solemn space. Beans, Tony, Carman, and Leia sat behind her. The attorney's voice carried a plea. "Look at her, your Honor, does she look like a flight risk?"

Weeks unraveled. A SOLD sign tilted in the Moretti's front yard. Rain poured over the shuttered puzzle store as a bank auctioneer called bids inside. Beans raised his hand with quiet confidence. Carman smirked.
"You think you're a pro now?"

Days later, Leia stood blindfolded on the sidewalk in a black dress. Carman and Beans sported dark suits with poorly looped ties. Beans tugged the cloth away from Leia's face, revealing the gleaming new sign: *Leia's Puzzles 'N More.* Her breath caught, hands flying to her face.
"Why?"
Beans smiled. "Family takes care of family."
She hugged him tight. "I don't know what to say, Chuckles."
"Don't make the kid jealous," he teased, nodding toward Carman.

Grief lingered. The house was still; the kind of silence that made every floorboard creak sound louder than it should. Beans and Chicky had bought time with a judge, but not for long. Wearing a black dress, Chicky moved slowly down the hallway, her hand gliding along the wallpaper as though she needed it to steady herself. She paused outside Tony's door, listening.

Inside, the faint glow of a lamp spilled across the room. Tony sat on the edge of his bed, in a faded dark-colored suit, hands working at the laces of his dress shoes, preparing for the long-overdue goodbye to Anna. He looked older than his years; the weight of responsibility slumped heavy across his shoulders. Chicky tapped lightly on the doorframe. "Can I come in?"
Tony glanced up, startled for a second, then nodded. "Yeah, Ma. Sure."

She stepped inside, closing the door gently behind her. The air in the room smelled faintly of aftershave and machine oil, a mixture that was uniquely Tony. She lowered herself onto the bed next to him, then tried desperately to tie his tie for him. "It's okay, Ma." He pulled the tie off. "I'll get it later."
"The only two women in your life leave you when you need them the most," she said softly.
Tony's guilt wore him like his cheap suit. He tried to tell his mentally fragile mother that her only son had betrayed her. But Chicky had her own thoughts to get out. Chicky tilted her head, her eyes tender, searching his face.
"You need to have someone in your life, Tony. The

most important decision we make in life is choosing who to spend it with."

"I'm fine," he muttered, reaching for the other shoe. There was a pause, and then her voice, quiet but steady:

"Did you know elephants mourn loss?" Her pained face stared at the mirror above his dresser. "And they can see themselves in a mirror."

"Huh."

"I don't anymore."

The words seemed to loosen something in him. He set the shoe down slowly, his hands lingering there before pulling back. He looked at her, his eyes tired, red at the edges.

"I blame myself," he said finally, his voice breaking slightly, and he swallowed hard. "I told the cops it was you, Ma. I'm so sorry."

He touched her hands gently, aching at her fragility. She kissed his palms.

"Promise me you'll make peace with your father."

He swallowed hard. "I told the cops it was you."

Her eyes softened. "How I loved when you giggled as a boy."

"I'm sorry, Ma. I had no choice." He buried his face in her shoulder. She only smiled, stroking his hair.

The confession hung heavy in the small room, pressing against both of them.

Chicky's eyes welled, but she reached for his hand, wrapping her frail fingers around his rough ones. "Tony... it wasn't your fault. You hear me? Not yours."

His shoulders shook, and he lowered his head. She leaned forward, kissing the top of his head like she had when he was a boy. The room was silent except for their breathing, mother and son bound together by grief, regret, and a love that neither time nor tragedy could break.

Love Never Forgets

The scent of lilies hung heavy in the air, thick and sweet, as if the flowers themselves were trying to soften the sharp edges of grief. At the front of D'Angelo's Funeral Home, a portrait of Anna Moretti smiled out from a forest of blooms — roses, carnations, orchids — all colors she loved. Her picture was framed in gold, the same light that used to gleam from her hair when the sun hit it just right.

Chicky stood before the photo, her hands trembling as she lit a candle. The tiny flame flickered, catching a glimmer of her tear-streaked face. She leaned forward and pressed her lips gently to the glass, the softest kiss of farewell.

Dominic's hand found hers. He helped her to her seat beside Tony, Carman, and Leia. Then, he made his way to the podium. His voice, familiar and gravelly, filled the quiet room.

"When Tony was little," Dominic began, "he used ta say to me, girls are for teasin'."

A few mourners chuckled, the laughter like fragile glass in the stillness.

"Then Beans told him, women carry men's seeds. And Tony said… like a garden?"

The laughter rippled again — gentle, grateful — even from Beans, who smiled through his tears.

"That ain't exactly—" Beans started, but Dominic waved him off.

"And when Tony got older and met Anna," Dominic

said softly, glancing at her portrait, "he told me I was wrong. Women make us better men."

He looked back toward Beans. "Fruit don't fall far from the tree, know what I'm sayin'?"

A tender murmur of agreement moved through the mourners.

Dominic drew a breath, his tone shifting, heavy now with truth. "Grief's a mother," he said. "When somebody we love gets sick, we get time ta accept it. Get ta say what needs ta be said. Like goodbye."

He looked out at the family — at Chicky, whose fingers were clutching a handkerchief to her lips, at Beans, sitting stiff and unblinking beside her.

"But when somebody dies quick… like Anna… there ain't that time," Dominic continued. "Just pain. So that's why I do this. Ta give my dear friend Beans, and his beautiful family, some closure."

He lifted a small cup of red wine from the podium, raising it high.

"To Anna," he said.

"To Anna," everyone echoed, voices breaking as they drank.

Chicky closed her eyes, letting the warmth of the wine spread through her chest. It was cathartic to finally say goodbye. It opened something in her mind that stress and grief had closed. Leia gave her a tender smile. Carman wrapped an arm around his father's shoulders. Beans exhaled — a long, trembling sigh — as Chicky's hand found his.

Outside, the summer rain was blunt and cold.

Black-clad mourners spilled from the funeral home, their murmurs rising like distant waves.

At the Moretti house, Tony stood by his car, his suit jacket wrinkled from hours of hugging. Beans helped an elderly mourner into her car, nodding absently as she thanked him. His eyes weren't really on her — they were fixed on Tony, who stared into the distance like a man half here, half somewhere else.

Chicky, watching from the living room window, clutched the puzzle box to her chest. The wood felt smooth beneath her trembling fingers, as though Anna's spirit was inside, trying to comfort her. Tears ran freely down her cheeks.

Beans approached Tony's car. Carman sat beside his father, his Pitt sweatshirt bright against the sea of black. Tony realized that his parents leaving town, as broken-hearted as he was, gave him space from the past and a future with Carman, regardless of where it was.

"I know Anna loved it," Tony said, nodding toward the service. "Thanks, Pop."

Beans forced a smile. "You need anything, Dominic's here." He turned to Carman. "You do good, huh? No Moretti ever made it through college."

Carman grinned. "I'll make us proud, Nonno."

Beans rubbed the back of Tony's neck affectionately, a gesture carrying years of unspoken love.

"You know I gotta do this," Beans said quietly. "They'll put her in an institution if we don't leave."

Tony nodded, eyes glistening. "You're doing the right

thing."

Carman leaned over. "Let us know you got there okay."

Beans nodded, his throat too tight for words.

Tony smiled faintly. "Yinz be careful. I hear it's pretty hot there—"

Beans leaned in, kissed his son's cheek. "I sent Marco the money from the house sale. He won't come after you."

Tony snorted. "He's a tool. Just be careful though." He jerked his chin toward a car down the block. "Ricco's got some unfinished business, it looks like."

Beans' gaze followed. Ricco sat in his car, a dark shape behind the windshield. Their eyes met for a second before Tony backed out of the driveway.

Beans watched the taillights disappear until there was nothing left but the whisper of the engine.

Inside, the house felt cavernous, hollowed out by grief. Beans loosened his tie as he entered. Chicky sat in her black dress, tears running silently down her face, the puzzle box in her lap.

"If I'd come home sooner that day…" she whispered.

Beans froze.

"I like this suit on you," she said, her tone lighter now, strange and familiar.

He walked to her, kissed her forehead, and began retying his own tie.

"I want the women on our flight to be jealous," she teased softly.

Beans' eyes watered. "I'll go get the suitcases."

As he turned toward the stairs, her voice followed:
"Don't forget your favorite razor's in the bathroom. And leave the key for the realtor."
He hesitated halfway up the steps. Something in her voice — sharp, clear, like the woman she once was — made him stop.
Then came a sound. Click. Click. Click.
Beans turned slowly. Chicky's trembling hands had lifted the lid of the puzzle box. Inside, the blade gleamed — the same knife that had once drawn blood and mystery.
Her eyes widened in wonder.
"Can we bring this on the plane?"
Beans' heart exploded with joy. He leapt down the stairs, sweeping her into his arms. They spun together, laughing, crying, the years of fear and loss dissolving in the sound of their laughter.

The old Chrysler eased down the driveway, sun flashing on its chrome. Inside, Beans and Chicky held hands, fingers intertwined. Behind them, Ricco's car followed at a distance.
When they passed Giacinta's Italian Cuisine, Beans honked and waved at Gia, who was standing by a bucket. She smiled sweetly — then dumped its contents, hundreds of cockroaches, onto Ricco's windshield as he passed behind them. His car swerved, jerking to a stop.
Beans caught the sight in his rearview mirror and chuckled, the first true laugh in months.

Hours later, a plane cut through the clouds, streaking toward the horizon painted in gold and rose. "Ladies and gentlemen," the pilot's voice announced, "we are about to touch down in Johannesburg."
Chicky stirred beside him, checking her seat belt. She reached over to adjust Beans', fussing like she always did. Then she noticed his tie, loose and crooked.
Beans opened his eyes, pretending to wake, smiling with deep, wordless gratitude. Her fingers moved with delicate precision, tying it just as she used to, back when mornings were filled with coffee and sunlight instead of pills and fear.
When she finished, he leaned in and kissed her cheek.

In the vast open wilds of South Africa, under the high blue sky, two figures rode side by side atop an elephant. Chicky's laughter echoed across the river, amidst the elephants that roamed nearby, majestic and free.
Beans held her close, his arm wrapped around her as if to protect her from the world. The knife from the puzzle box hung harmlessly at his belt — a relic now, not a threat.
Ahead of them, a herd of elephants moved through the water, their great bodies shimmering in the light. And for the first time in a long, long while, Beans felt whole.
The knife gleamed, a strange reminder of everything they had lost — and everything they had managed to hold onto. Together, they rode forward — toward memory, toward love, toward whatever time remained.

Epilogue

The Garden Remembered

The sun was low over the plains, gold light spilling across the tall grass like something divine. From above, they must have looked small — two specks swaying gently on the back of an elephant, moving steadily toward the river's bend.
Beans rested his chin on Chicky's shoulder. Her hair, silver now but still soft as silk, caught the wind. The years had been cruel to them, but not unkind in this moment — not here, where time seemed to loosen its grip.

For a long while, neither spoke. The only sound was the rustle of the elephant's ears and the far-off cry of a bird. Then Chicky sighed, the kind that holds a hundred stories in one breath.
"It's beautiful," she whispered.
"It is," he said. "You picked a good place."
She smiled faintly. "Did I?"
Beans nodded, pressing a kiss against her temple.
"Yeah. You always do."
She looked ahead, at the water gleaming like glass.
"Do you think Anna can see us?"
Beans didn't answer right away. He let the question hang in the warm air, like incense. "I think she's right here," he said finally. "All around us. Maybe in that bird. Maybe in that river. Maybe in this crazy

elephant."
Chicky laughed softly — the same light, musical laugh that used to float through their kitchen while sauce simmered on the stove.
"She'd like that," she said.
"Yeah," he whispered. "She would."

As the elephant lumbered onward, Beans reached into his pocket and pulled out the puzzle box — smooth now from her constant handling. The lid, once impossible to open, slid easily beneath his thumb. Inside was nothing but air.
He smiled. The mystery was never in the box — it was in the living, in the remembering.
He let the box fall into the river. The water took it gently, carrying it downstream, catching the sun in its polished wood one last time before it disappeared beneath the current.
Chicky turned to him. "What was in it?"
"Everything that mattered," he said. "And nothin' that does."
She leaned against him, her hand finding his. Together they watched the river shimmer and wind away, endless as memory.

Above them, the sky deepened from gold to violet. The elephants moved on, slow and sure, into the heart of the setting sun.

www.ingramcontent.com/pod-product-compliance
Lightning Source LLC
Chambersburg PA
CBHW071540100726
47908CB00004B/1447